BEYOND

The Frozen Future

Preface

Let us take you on a journey you'll never forget - gasp, sweat, scream, smile and laugh together. Futuristic fiction created to entertain, thought-provoke and stimulate readers with unique dynamism and imagination. Tantalizing characters, plausible future worlds and gripping plots you will fall in love with.

Inspired by her engineering roots and investment career, Ema Cory brings unique creativity and perspective to invent an immersive and unforgettable journey for her global audience.

Acknowledgment

I would firstly like to thank the Comic Book industry for igniting my passion for imagination and encouraging different ways of thinking. I greatly appreciate the authors, artists and creators who I've reached out to for their warmth and wisdom. The Disney Classic films also taught me the importance of script and pace for creating moving experiences.

I would also like to thank my incredible parents, who without their love and support I would not have the stomach (or any other organs in fact!) to write a book. My soul mate, my husband, was so instrumental in getting this launched that I'll be forever grateful - thank you again for everything and being the light in my life.

I wasn't expecting to write this, but thank you to all those who I've worked with in the Investment industry who gave me the insight into highly different personalities and ambitions that are core themes in this book. My other influencers include Al Gore (such a big fan!), Densel Washington and Arnie (your motivational speeches really moved me), and Sheryl

Sandburg and Bethenny Frankel (such great books) who taught me a lack of action is not an option.

The biggest thank you of all though, is to you dear reader! Let me take you on an adventure; Beyond was more than a simple passion for story writing - I wanted to capture so many extreme forces that we face today which can be exciting but also terrifying and will impact future generations. The real reason for launching this book is to provide a stimulating and exciting read that is fully immersive and thought provoking in an entertaining and deeply unique way. Therefore please do read with an open mind and prepare to be immersed in The Frozen Future!

Table of Contents

ACT 1 — 9

THE EARTH WAS A FORMLESS VOID AND DARKNESS COVERED THE FACE OF THE DEEP — 12

AND THERE WAS EVENING, AND THERE WAS MORNING — 16

LET THERE BE A DOME IN THE MIDST OF THE WATERS, AND LET IT SEPARATE THE WATERS FROM THE WATERS — 21

LET THERE BE LIGHT — 29

ACT 2 — 37

THE GREATER LIGHT TO RULE THE DAY AND THE LESSER LIGHT TO RULE THE NIGHT — 38

LET THE WATERS UNDER THE SKY BE GATHERED TOGETHER INTO ONE PLACE, AND LET THE DRY LAND APPEAR — 45

LET THE WATERS BRING FORTH SWARMS OF LIVING CREATURES — 52

EVERYTHING THAT CREEPS UPON THE
GROUND OF EVERY KIND   55

ACT 3   61
YOU SHALL HAVE THEM FOR FOOD   62
ONLY, YOU SHALL NOT EAT FLESH WITH ITS
LIFE, THAT IS, ITS BLOOD   65
AND IT WAS SO   67
IN THE BEGINNING   71
BE FRUITFUL AND MULTIPLY, AND FILL THE
EARTH   78
LET THEM HAVE DOMINION OVER THE FISH
OF THE SEA, AND OVER THE BIRDS OF THE
AIR, AND OVER THE CATTLE, AND OVER ALL
THE WILD ANIMALS OF THE EARTH, AND
OVER EVERY CREEPING THING THAT CREEPS
UPON THE EARTH   87
WHOEVER SHEDS THE BLOOD OF A HUMAN;
BY A HUMAN SHALL THAT PERSON'S BLOOD
BE SHED   92

Copyright © 2020 Ema Cory

All rights reserved. No part of this book may be reproduced in any form on by any electronic or mechanical means, including information storage and retrieval systems, without permission in writing from the publisher, except by a reviewer who may quote brief passages in a review.

This is a work of fiction. Names, characters, places and incidents either are the product of the author's imagination or are used fictitiously. Any resemblance to actual persons, living or dead, events, or locales is entirely coincidental.

www.emacory.com

ACT 1

CHAPTER 1

The earth was a formless void and darkness covered the face of the deep

The air was charged with anticipation. The hall hummed with unanswered questions. The seats were all filled below a cloud of drones balancing live streaming cameras over their propellers, which frequently clashed against one another. The students salivated at the thought of another rousing debate. Today was a record turnout, fewer had turned up nearly 20 years ago at the outbreak of World War III "should Ivy League students be exempt from Duty?" This was a different call of duty.

Every 4 years democracy stands the test in the US. Which president will serve for the greatest honor; the greatest demand; the greatest job in the world? Throughout 2279 several sex scandals, non-fake news and just sheer bad PR had caused not only both leading candidates but also their back-ups and even their back-ups to drop out of the presidential race. The vast dearth of suitable alternatives threw the country into chaos and confusion like flamingos on ice.

Tommy had promised to reveal an exciting solution for the nation. The rugged, short and stout student approached the podium, dragging his feet. Despite the dirty, wild black hair overpowering the intense facial expression and deep brown eyes, Tommy commanded the presence of a room like no other. Completely unattractive but completely captivating, he had enemies and friends in equal amounts yet influenced them all seamlessly under his spell. While a farmer's son, the heir to the largest cattle farm in Texas didn't eat much humble pie.

All mouths closed shut and eyes directed to the front of the stage. Pupils were poised on the edge of seats, the silence was tantalizingly teasing and Tommy knew it. The electricity even made his untamed hair stick up a couple of inches more. He licked his large bulging lips and began. Raising his head to show the wild eyes and project his great, grand and deliberately slow paced voice:
"Friends and fellow students – I bring you the solution to our leadership crisis in this 2279 election" in the audience mouths opened, eyes focused and the cameras on the drones focused acutely. They all smelt change unwinding here today.

"History repeats itself – We have seen too many wars start the same way, too many financial crises with clear warning signs and too many politicians fail us again and again." He slowly leant into the podium, raising a single hand while clasping the podium with the other

"Therefore I argue our future is not in front of us... but rather in the past" all Yale students were confused. However university had granted them sufficient practice in maintaining their cool and unflustered composure while being completely unaware of what's going on in front of them.

"In 2017 we had similar challenges to that of today – immigrants plaguing our streets, unfair unemployment and terrorism – and they were solved by the one and only Tomp." Roars erupted. Hands clapped violently. Heads nodded in approval. Only a few glanced wildly at their neighbors in shock.

Tommy quickened his pace and shouted above the furor "He is currently frozen in London in the custody of 'Life Beyond' – I say we awake him to lead us through these troubles again!" Releasing the podium his arms flung high in the air like a winning athlete, although his sweat patches were even greater than a long-distance runner. The puppeteer had only just begun. "Wake up Tomp" his minions chanted, scattered equally across the chamber for impact and rapidly evolved into "Wakeup Tomp. Wakeup Tomp" the chant echoed until it became a synchronized demand. Everyone knew what part they must now play to solve the crisis; make noise, make demands for we must bring forth the logical solution – bring back a hero who stayed true to their words.

CHAPTER 2

And there was evening, and there was morning

On the other side of the pond the sun was retiring for the day. London's skyline transformed every other week. New skyscrapers replaced old ones deemed unsuitable by the ever-present police surveillance whilst increasing the volume of real estate stock. Safety had to be prioritized after 200 years of 'imminent' terror alert.

The smog on the other hand was a permanent feature, lined by a swarm of drones and their red blinking lights. In the haste to upgrade the area architects replicated models and layouts, creating an unimaginative Lego-like grid. The roads were narrow, with hovering automated vehicles speeding along delivering bulk goods too large for teleportation or drones. Preciously protected with electrified wiring or spikes, the homeless dared not interfere. Their mouths were constantly open like fish catching oxygen in a toxic sea. Some were environmental refugees, some asylum seekers, but most were the redundant and unemployed who were not able to save more than a month's pay in their lifetime. Employers were getting desperate; they would convince staff they had been paid through a simple computer screenshot, but somehow the wage payment was lost in transition like when the teleportation goes wrong. At least those on the streets felt the rain; saw the sun through the drone cloak and to a very limited extent through the smog to the beautiful night sky. This was more than most who experience the luxury high-rise high-pressure existence.

The CEO and majority shareholder of Life Beyond, the distinguished Body Freezing London based organization, Alison Greshwood was trying to recall the last time she slept. Her mind was then drifting to when she even had her last period, as her body was out of sync with nature and reality in so many ways. She knew this zombie state would pass and her control freak normative state return but for now she needed to be alone and relax. It was a Sunday after all. She placed her soft ivory skin under the shower. Purified ice-cold water gently enveloped her, a protective cocoon. Alison had the eyes of an angel, ocean blue with long black eyelashes. Her manicured slim fingernails ran through her short blond and perfectly cut hair that covered her tiny ears and forehead with soft fringe. Almost pixie like, her slender frame was supported by long straight legs or as the media wrote 'endless legs that you could...'. It was a miracle what science could do in this time. For a premium price one could find cures for bags under the eyes, thinning hair, stomach ulcers, eye twitching, bad posture, short and quick breathing, but not for inner peace.

She still didn't like what she saw in the floor length mirror. She saw through the feminine features and delicate beauty. Staring back at her was what she never wanted to be. Someone she was ashamed of. She may have scratches on her forearms and tops of her legs, but she saw the deeper scars that haunted her.

Stepping through the body-drier - a thin barrier between the shower and bathroom blasting hot air for instant drying - she took her medication and slipped into her pale pink silk pajama, which were almost as weightless as her. As routine dictates, she poured a whisky from the decanter.

Alison's apartment was one of the highest specification blocks in Westminster. She lived alone in the over spacious three bedroom, four bathroom flat decorated by the most esteemed interior designers in a white and light blue haven. She had purged the place of any mementos of Scott, replicating the same exercise she did with mementos of her father all those years ago. Why do men always let her down she sighed to herself. It took several hours to wipe all the wedding preparation files from her e-pad. The electronic photos displayed TIME magazine front covers of 'CEO of the year', cut outs of the '30 under 30', 'most influential women' lists and 'Life Beyond back in the black' articles of her miraculous turnaround of the family firm. She kept every article of her momentous achievement – a new and insanely modern freeze facility. This and Italian Renaissance art dominated the apartment. There were no group friend shots; after all there was not enough time for work, and Scott, let alone friends.

Suddenly she was accompanied by an almost deafening news alert. Alison turned her head and half closed eyes on the plump sofa towards the wall that read "Breaking News – Body Freezing Related". American personality Carlson was summarizing Tommy's speech displaying those famous pearly white tiny teeth "With the Republican Party in disarray after a wave of scandals, Yale students are proposing a dramatic measure: To awaken a previous president from Freezing – Tomp. A petition has gained traction with an astounding 9 million US signatures". Alison sat up in alarm like a charmed cobra. Her hands were shaking around her head. Tears gently streamed. "Fucking fantastic," she muttered with gritted teeth and now red blood shot eyes. As routine dictates, she finished the decanter.

CHAPTER 3

Let there be a dome in the midst of the waters, and let it separate the waters from the waters

Lucy was the youngest Head of Research at any Body Freezing facility by far, and boy did she know it. She carried that characteristic smug and proud expression wherever she went. Her tall masculine frame strutted wide shoulders and hips covered with piercings and ink. Her feline facial features were framed by spikey red flamed hair, barely covering her crawling neck tattoos. Her deep brown eyes were sharp, her narrow lips bent upwards but only at the very edges. London born and bred, her US education had gifted her with a distinct accent that had shocked the narrow UK Body Freezing community. No other country had developed the systems and technology as far, with Life Beyond founded in Cambridge in 2055 as the first firm to successfully do so at scale.

There were no awards to be won in this industry. No bonuses. Not even a summer event or Christmas party. No team bonding was needed. Her fulfilment was the work itself. Lucy's sole ambition was to be the first in the world to successfully wake up a frozen body. Not so she could leap through the future herself, but to be one of the few who made a meaningful claim in this shallow world; to control time itself. She knew Life Beyond was the first place to achieve this and now she was here, in the top job. It was only a matter of time.

A culture shock would be one description of her first month at the family firm. Her research team consisted of twenty people. That's right, twenty. Not the 125 she had been leading before. Every single member had a hunched back from bending down over bodies or freeze pods, although Lucy observed more time was spent completing forms than anything else. After all, the revenue from selling research to healthcare and pharmaceutical companies drove the company bottom line just as much as the new customer joining fees.

While Alison lead the company under a firm hand, she hadn't exactly warmed to Lucy in the interview. Her predecessor Dr Thomas had slipped in the shower and while over 7,000 applied to fill his shoes only 3,000 didn't need work visas to join and 100 had the necessary skills. Lucy was a wild card, but Alison felt a change was needed in the suffocating pristine firm.

Day in day out, the 2,000 employees come to work; 1,000 in the finance department, 700 sales, 20 researchers and the rest security and admin. The finance team consisted of investors managing the savings of the Frozen customers for an ever so non-modest annual fee and bailiffs collected payments from customers who had used the 'friends installment program' or essentially 'pass off the annual fees to relatives'. The sales staff reached out to numerous demographics; youths searching for a new playground, the middle aged in dead end jobs who might as well be frozen, older generations looking for health solutions as life expectancy had stalled at 90 years.

13 years ago Alison revolutionized the firm with the new freezing facility, and simultaneously cut the number of staff by over half. Praised as an innovator, the media were kind and the masses followed like sheep to put her on a pedestal. Sympathy also played a part in this given the circumstances in which she inherited the firm. Alison's aura of success commanded respect from all those in her presence.

Lucy, however, was an exception to the rule. Full of her own importance, tensions could be felt within miles of the two highly educated, highly paid and highly ambitious women. Several weeks ago during the daily inspection Lucy, from her perspective, gently approached Alison in a professional manner to simply ask that non-current diseases research be dropped and resources focused elsewhere. Alison, from her perspective however, saw an aggressive figure marching towards her commanding change for the sake of it to assert her dominance, which somehow she felt had been earned through being born with broader shoulders. There was only one solution - humiliate and put her in her place - move the argument to an open battleground and throw her a formal warning for inappropriate behavior. What a first month.

Lucy teleported from her flat into the pristine brightly lit white lab. There were four teams;
- NCD - Analysis of those who died within Life Beyond's care with 'non-current' or curable diseases. The resultant research papers were the best form of marketing, cementing the firm as an industry leader with deep and thorough research skills.

- CD - analysis of those who died with current diseases. Results were sold to the highest corporate bidder.
- BR - Bioresearch and freezing fluid development. Their USP or 'secret sauce', this lab was heavily fortified and was Lucy's primary focus. How was this not always working? How did some diseases continue to mutate when frozen?
- Technology - developing systems to upgrade the body-pods.

The CD team, as always, were early birds - hunched over a body chatting about some chick-flick casually while slowing tearing up a translucent bloated corpse. Their fingers meticulously hovered over a computer screen that subsequently guided the shiny and slim robotic knives effortlessly through the body. Chuan, Gabriella and Arjun didn't notice Lucy's arrival. Their light grey plain uniform had Aztec blue, green and yellow design features around the narrow edges and wide collar. Lucy coughed. No response. They were too engrossed in their work and chat. Lucy put on the tight latex light blue medical gloves with a loud 'snap'. Their faces swiveled in silence. That's better, Lucy thought.

"So another one bites the dust?" Lucy breathed out, tired already at 8am.

"Looks like Fluid 2165 V2 has reacted with the liver" Chan pointed swiftly to the screen and then carved out a small mutation from the abdomen without appearing to blink or even breathe.

"Perfectly created" he muttered, always amazed at the simultaneous robustness and fragility of the human body.

Gabriella announced with gusto "This is the third one from that freezing fluid, all had history of alcohol abuse so we'll need to run the full diagnostics." She barely reached the operating table at 4ft. However her 5ft width gave her sufficient lung capacity to be heard loud and clear, even in the adjacent lab. Her bug-like eyes pushing against her glasses always creeped Lucy out; Were they bulging because the glasses were too tight or were they really that big and just pushing out the glass lenses?

"Alison has asked for a report by end of day" Gabriella proudly announced. Lucy felt her stomach clench, why does everyone report to Alison first and not the new Head of Research?

Calmly with tight lips she paced herself "We run to our timetable not hers. We can't keep accepting clients if 6% are dying in our custody"

With an almost joyous expression Arjun couldn't resist "Well she's the boss... has been for over 12 years" a unified smile glistened across the teams faces, waiting for Lucy's response. They knew any 'inappropriate behavior' or comment would be her last warning. She could be booted out on her grubby young heels by the end of the quarter.

Lucy, as always, left angry, her face almost as red as her hair, "Those old bastards need to remember who they are speaking to for fuck's sake, who do they think they are? Keep calm, keep calm, just focus on what's important – it'll be your face in the media once you wake someone up, no one else's" she screamed in her head.

CHAPTER 4

Let there be light

Alison wore her usual white sleeveless short tight dress, long full arm-length white gloves and a glamorous dark blue African print silk scarf cascading over her left shoulder and draping down her arm. Style and modern professionalism emanated from this pale figure. She approached Chamber 12, the first of 10 that Monday morning. She stopped in the bleach white corridor next to a dark grey 12 sign as tall as her. Jack was bending down reading the pad, for the first time Alison noticed a bald patch in his grey haired head. He whispered in his usual delicate soft spoken manner "Michael Blatt, 78, Jewish. Here with only son Abraham and daughter in law Mary who are paying through our installments program. We are using freeze Fluid 2279 V5 until muscular regeneration can regrow his whole right leg back."

He tucked the pad away and opened the purple box with great care. Alison's hand paused over the Star of David gold brooch, one of the seven items in the box. She smiled in admiration at those who can see what doesn't meet the eye, an idea that there is so much more. Her grandfather taught her the importance of respecting other beliefs, after all that's what a good Christian would do. Trouble is she wasn't a very good Christian, or even a good one. There were only 10 commandments yet she struggled with nearly all of them;

- Don't have any other Gods – well quite frankly, money had become her priority. With no home ownership under the new Global Home Organisation every single person was only a few pay cheques away from sucking oxygen on the polluted streets and become excluded from the rationing systems. Survival, by definition, comes before afterlife.
- Thou shall not take the Lord's name in vain – well sort of, does swearing only to yourself count?
- Remember to keep the Sabbath day Holy – there really is no rest for the wicked, with new customers arriving 7 days a week it's hard to keep track of time.
- Honor thy mother and father – How on earth could I? My father? The one who drove the family legacy into debt and ruin? The alcoholic loser who left me alone at 18 with all this?

- Thou shall not kill – Ha! Well that's a tough one. Life Beyond freezes at least 10 people a day, promising a wake up call in a perfect future yet we have never woken anyone up successfully, in fact we have a 10% annual death rate. The pyramid scheme only works if sales keep up. I'm making my living by stopping life, or ending it. A haunting idea I prefer not to think about.
- Thou shall not commit adultery, thou shall not steal, thou shall not bear false witness – well I don't have a problem with that but why do others? I've tried to love as I would want to be loved but it didn't seem to work out. I should have known better with Scott.

"What happened to his leg" Alison casually queried?
Jack looked her straight in the eye "it was blown off in the war, I think he was in Nigeria if I recall". He swiped a hand near the door, an invisible barrier disappeared and the door opened.
Alison confidently pronounced "Michael – a pleasure to meet you and your family." As routine dictated, her warm smile and open arms surprised the new customers.

The family of three was sitting down in the light green waiting room on plush sofas, the calming classical music gently playing in the background. They were all emaciated. Michael looked like death already, although the prosthetic leg was incredibly life-like.

His large skeletal frame was held in the grey Life Beyond robe, matching the color of his well maintained hair. Balanced at the end of his long slender neck, his striking face projected oddly forward, not stooping like most of his age. His deep brown eyes protected by bushy brows were engaged and aflame with anger, regret, fear and sadness all at once. No one could empathize with the horrors of war he had witnessed. The lack of fulfillment of soldier promises had made the world sick and distrustful. No one knew what they were really defending. How can you define civilization and mankind? Michael knew that today was the end, and while planned and in full control the reality was that the decision might as well have been made for him.

"I would like to thank you and your family for selecting Life Beyond for such an important journey. We are proud to be the leading innovator in pausing time" waiting for her message to sink in, she noticed

Michael was shaking in fear with small beads of sweat across his brow. His son Abraham was firmly holding his hand like a wheel on an uncontrollable car although was holding back some tears himself.

"And also extend my gratitude for saving our nation in the World War." This was a sincere comment. The War had impacted so many globally; all of her extended family had suffered injuries that could not be fixed. Her favorite cousin Gerald only returned as a head, it could have been wired up to a new body but the thought freaked out her father who had simply pulled the life-support plug. Spineless bastard.

"Will he feel any pain Ms. Greshwood?" Mary's eyes were laser focused as she sat like a cat in a state of readiness. While she was surprised the CEO was visiting them, her priority was her father in-law's safety. This freezing business wasn't her idea but her husband's, causing several heated emotional arguments at home. While not a blood-relative, Michael was so much to so many people in their community.

"While we try to minimize any discomfort, there will be a mild sting for a few seconds. My trusted clinicians will take you through to the chamber with your selected Rabbi" The family looked at each other simultaneously in a magical deeply connected moment. They seemed to be saying everything they needed in one heart-felt look. Mary kissed his head and Abraham hugged his father so tightly his bones almost crushed.

As Alison left the waiting room, two clinicians dressed in dark grey long dresses and gloves took Michael through to the freezing chamber and made him sign one last form one last time before removing the robe.

The shiny white casket had light green padding. Ice-cold nano-needles pressed into Michael's skin slowly as the Rabbi read the last rights. He could hear Mary crying in the room next door. Was he making the right decision? The thought of not seeing Mary and Abraham again was heartbreaking and painful, how could that be weighed against the everyday throbbing of his lost leg? Before he could change his mind the clinicians calmly with respect closed the casket and sealed it shut with a button.
"Freezing initiated" the computer showed a progress bar shooting up to 100% within 2 seconds. The fluid pipe was removed and casket rolled through to 'the fridge'.

Alison was pacing up the corridor to chamber 9 with Jack reading "Tessa Harding, 82, atheist, here alone…"

ACT 2

CHAPTER 5

The greater light to rule the day and the lesser light to rule the night

It wasn't the first Monday of every quarter but interesting times had called for a meeting. Alison took the lift from the 55th floor to ground, the storage area. Whenever she enters the lift she fondly recalls the media spin on her office being on the 55th floor, exactly in the middle of the 110th story building "the CEO in touch with her company, right in the heart of the action" whereas the reality was there was no view from 55 upwards just smog! She was amused the 'bigger is better' mentality spanned to almost everything in the industries run by men!

Her security waited by the door astutely. All seven men were over 7ft tall, in black gothic industrial plastic like cloaks with wide, sharp and spikey black metal across the shoulders. The red shiny gas masks covered their whole faces. The funny chemical smell scared yet strangely calmed her.

Alison scanned the ID cards, she knew all the men were previous African spies handpicked from life jail sentences to serve as her security. She only hoped they always stayed on her side. The silent brigade prepared for the perilous walk. The Wild West catchphrase was well versed. This afternoon Alison wore a grey jumpsuit with pearl strands draping from tightly around her long white neck to loosely over her waist. The thick black coat with sharp oversized hood was placed on her, a weight she could barely stand. The light green gas mask was fitted across her face with a few tests conducted for safety. Too many people depended on her.

Facing the door the silent brigade took their places. One led with two just behind, two at her sides tethered to her arms and two guarded from behind. Too much was at risk. The cattle rods with barbed wire came out. Electrified rods were now banned so they had to make do. As the gate opened an alien dusty light came through. The masks lit up bright red and green. "All Clear" with eight light bars coming up on the screens, they had acclimatized to the Westminster outdoors territory.

All systems were go; They power walked left, the one at the front waving the rod fiercely across the sea of homeless, all reaching out in desperation; not specifically for food, or water, or clothes or money, but some pity or any form of help. They overflowed in the streets, turning violent quite frequently. The front leader directed the other four protectors while those beside Alison held her fragile frame up in the heavy outwear gear preventing any other form of human contact. She always kept her eyes closed. They clubbed anyone who reached out nearby. Some were thrown onto the roads for the vehicles to deal with. The screaming and deafening whirling noise of hovercrafts speeding by was like a warzone.

Walking always seemed a strange concept, both unnatural and primitive at the same time in the automation era. After an hour Alison arrived exhausted. "Welcome to the Goring" the staff carefully removed her gear and escorted her to the ladies. Her legs were like jelly as she almost fell down the stairs. She remained seated on the couch for 10 minutes gaining strength to stand again and collected her thoughts for the meeting. As her grandfather would say "Keep your friends close, and the politicians closer. Fuck your enemies left right and center".

Alison approached the beautiful Dining Room; all 20 antique tables were filled by security guards, with her drinking companion sat at the center table; The only

customer, although he looked anything other than lonely. Amed filled the chair with his oversized plump physique, the fattest man in town. The Bangladeshi was an example of the UK dream, an immigrant benefitting from being at the right place at the right time, climbing the political ladder without any charisma, skill or intellect. Democracy had been kind to him for three terms, only because he was the only Bangladeshi in politics.
"My favorite CEO" he wasn't lying
"My favorite Prime Minster" she was, she hated these meetings but knew they were important.
"So how have you been, I haven't seen you since er.. since two weeks ago?" Alison was still recovering from 'the best day of her life '20 May 2279'....

She should have seen the signs with Scott; spoke only about himself, limited eye contact during sex, changed jobs more times than underwear and had proposed a few weeks after the rich list was published. She just wanted to be loved and was sick of being alone. They had argued leading up to the wedding; Alison wanted it to be in a church. She had entered the glass-vaulted hall filled with the London elite yet the music didn't start. The Best Man charged up the aisle with a mumbled whisper "I'm s...so.. sorry, Scott...lets go over here". The coward had bolted at the last minute back to his ex-slut. Alison later attempted a cowardly act, leaning in a drunken state over the balcony before crying backwards onto the floor shaking from lack of oxygen.

"It's been tough but I've been alright, made of sturdy stuff! I'm just getting straight back into work now". She needed to work far more than the company needed her.

Amed wasn't the best with emotions, or logic for that matter. But he had a good heart and tried to reach out to Alison's hand that was on the base of the wine glass. Like a rabbit approaching a tiger, the hand reached for a gentle pat gesture. Alison was startled and made a small jump. His hand swiftly retracted.

Embarrassed, he quickly changed the subject to the matter at hand "I need to talk to you about this Tomp business" he looked around the room. Not sure what he was looking for, there was only security but anyone could be dangerous.
"Dawson Tomp, the distant relative, is coming to London… THIS Thursday"

Alison nearly spat out her wine but composed herself by leaning back on the chair with her arms closed, pressing against the cold pearls.

"I've said it before and I'll say it again – we can't have anyone waking up yet" Amed's tone had shifted from concern to anger. He was flustered and dogmatic.

"The Global Food Organization is cutting our rations – seven China plantations were deemed too toxic and have been closed down". While he is the prime minister important resources such as food, water, waste, housing and transportation were all managed by global organizations outside his control. World War III started with a small number of African nations resisting globalization. With populations swelling and space declining it was for survival. North Korea had teamed up with China to resist, but as punishment these nations were put under 'zero child policy' with their races expected to die out over the next 30 years.

"The UK has too many mouths to feed – we took in 10 million climate refugees alone last year and 4 million terrorism related. If we wake up Tomp we will be deemed 'elitist' and other counties will ask for their politicians to be released - we CANNOT be caught up in that."

Out of breath he confessed, "I've admired your company and leadership, I'll do what I can but you need to hold firm and resist this wave of pressure."

Amed needed Alison just as much as she needed him. Her calm composure masked her desire to hug him in thanks; no one could be woken up. It hadn't been done and it was far too dangerous. Over 12,000 freezing fluids had been developed and each had at least one death under custody. It was a relief the reporting requirements had reduced.
"It will come thick and fast I warn you" his stubby hand pointing in the air. A shiver went up Alison's spine. She needed to devise a plan for Thursday.

CHAPTER 6

Let the waters under the sky be gathered together into one place, and let the dry land appear

Immediate action was required. Alison returned to the office. As rain drizzled down the pristine glass tower casting a gentle ticking noise, time was running out. Alison approached her pride and glory - 'the fridge' facility. There were 7 sets of computer and human visual security checks. After years in the technology game, glitches and potential hacks were a risk not worth taking when it came to security. Security checks carried out by man, not machine, were certainly preferred. There was only one way in, and one way out of 'the fridge facility'.

World War III made all developed, emerging, Eastern and Western nations surrender to master global organizations claiming to save humanity from low resources by managing these fairly on their behalf. The War had left many scars. Graham, Alison's father, was adamant that surviving wounded soldiers should not be on the streets but be prioritized for all security roles. The welfare system had failed, that was a global decision. Discrimination was not allowed in any organization but Alison didn't care – ex-soldiers always made it straight through to the final interview stages at Life Beyond.

Luke, an overly keen overly ambitious workman in light blue overalls, proudly opened the last door. While he was trying to display to the single 30-year-old multi-millionaire his impressive muscles, Alison glided straight through blissfully unaware of his efforts. She grinned with pride as she entered. The colossal central area had over 10 storage facilities protected with light green garage like shutter doors on each side of the cube up all five stories. One side however was a glass walled analysis unit. When an individual pod detected a malfunction, a handyman would investigate immediately, moving the pod to the secure analysis center via the lifts in the unit. Either the fluid would be topped up, changed, pod fixed or circuit replaced, or as in most cases the body be removed and taken to the research team through the main entrance / exit. The facility was otherwise bright, light, clinical and completely functional. However there were no security cameras and access to the fridge was strictly limited. The handymen here had to prove themselves with over 20 year's experience at the firm before being allowed to interview for these heart and soul positions at Life Beyond.

Several handymen were finishing for the day, vacantly dragging their feet towards the exit. No teleportation units were allowed – one walking entrance only, the easiest to monitor. One-way in, one-way out. The front of every storage facility could be seen from the central screens, the only request to the designers. All steel shutters were securely closed with glowing green circles on the side. Not only did 'the fridge' fit the function of the units, with the freezing fluid keeping millions of individuals in an ageing-free slumber until the promised better future, but the facility also happened to be cold due to its vast scale.

Whatever the hour, you could count on trusted Billy to be there. Billy was the longest serving employee, the only one to receive a Christmas bonus. He was also the oldest at 113 years old but knew how to work all the systems inside out. Originally an immigrant from Bangladesh who had lost his home like millions to flooding, Life Beyond was where he belonged for the last 80 years.

He was head of the Storage Units as they were known under both James (Alison's grandfather) and Graham (Alison's father). He had witnessed Graham proudly showing off a bouncing little blond bundle around the office, taught the spotty geeky teenager how the system works, wept and drank with a mourning daughter and guided one of the youngest CEOs on people management. Billy was special to the Greshwoods, always had been and always would be. His 10-person team religiously followed the daily drills from 8am to 7pm prompt. There were no cleaners or other staff, everything was self-cleaning, all technology systems wheeled in and out the one door. Billy, his 10 workers and Alison were the only ones permitted in 'the fridge'. Lucy had tried to rename as 'the morgue' but this never caught on.

Alison's heels chimed against the shinning white floor, the delicate echo resounded across the entire space. While well lit the atmosphere was bleak and air thin. She approached Billy and the central machine with a clear purpose.
"Carlson Tomp is coming on Thursday. Tomp was a 2055 vintage". They both let in a difficult deep breath and nodded to each other. Eye contact was enough. No words were exchanged. They knew this day would come and had their plan in place.

Quickening her pace Alison almost jogged back to her grey office. Alison inhaled the silent still air. The grey walls were built from thick slabs of grey and white lined marble, deadening any sound and furthermore restricting any form of internet or outside connection. The walls were lined with the occasional floor to ceiling length mirror and portraits. The only furnishings were her marble desk, her own chair (there was never a chair for guests – they had to stand, it made for much shorter meetings) and each corner of the room was occupied with a unique wooden antique African totem pole. Somehow these overseeing ornaments made her feel safe, with the bonus of making her guests feel spooked. The unimaginative room was perfectly square, the 30ft tall heavy door opened to face Alison's desk square on, with a view of the London skyline beyond. The 30ft tall window looked out onto the melting raindrops blurring the view. This was still her favorite view. The other walls were lined with larger than life-size family portraits;

- Dr Philip - founder of Life Beyond, a crazy academic who won several Nobel prizes for advancing the field of Body Freezing. His obnoxious hyena like laugh was almost as infamous as his work.

- Dr Philip Junior - his son saw the competition coming and changed the culture from that of open sharing to secrecy. Cultivating an almost mystical image. There was no more working relationships with universities but a suspicious in-house team.
- Daisy - responded to the competition by establishing a sales team and realizing the importance of connections, threw lavish parties for politicians, opening a dialogue on an otherwise ignored industry. She winked at everyone with a cheeky grin. In an effort to rebrand the company the logo changed from black and white 'LIFE BEYOND' to the blue one used today.
- James - was a charismatic character. A true leader. With a big belly and big ideas he took the company public, raising billions. Then realizing this involved a lot of paperwork and reporting 10 years later he took it private again, and was still praised by the finance world for his brilliance. This had introduced corporate debt for the first time.
- Graham - was the black sheep. Completely out of his depth, his alcohol addiction along with the debt swelled. He burst the bubble by popping too many pills. Leaving three failed marriages and a daughter he left no note. No will. Barely a trace. Alison had found him when she came back from dinner, an hour after coming into the flat. The press were not kind

about him, even an ex tried to release a sex tape but who on earth would pay to see that bloated body wobbling around!

Alison couldn't bear to look at these. Each one had a clear legacy, all good, except for her father. While she had banked some points through restructuring the debt, reshaping the company, bringing it back to the number one Body Freezing provider and installing 'the fridge' facility she knew that would be more than offset by future revelations. The music would have to stop. Until then the future is blotted out by the hum of busyness and drink. She poured another whisky and sat at her designer desk. Pacing her breathing to slow down her heart rate an hour passed. She checked the systems. They were good to go.

CHAPTER 7

Let the waters bring forth swarms of living creatures

All senses were distorted in Reid's. Music pounded through every fiber of every body, shaking heads to the rhythm of the night. Smoke blurred sights, but everyone came to see the men dancing on stage around the props. Incense mixed with sweat and hormones created a confused clammy smell and taste. Everything was sticky, the wide wooden chairs, the floor, the glasses filled with cheap and dubious liquor, everything melted into the ground. Women went to be indulged but came out in an almost deprived state. This was Lucy's hangout.

In the darkened center of the club Rwanda in a drunken, drugged state of sloth sprawled out in a wooden chair. Most joints and limbs were limp; Her mouth hung open and arms drooped off the chair arms (brushing past her best friend Lucy). Lucy was sitting upright in her black leather jeans and nothing but a black fringe suede scarf preserving her modesty. She liked having her back and neck tattoos

on display. Her facial piercing was in as soon as she clocked off from work. Her height and wild eyes always made her stand out from the crowd yet the dancers were too scared to come too close. While a 6ft tall emaciated yet toned man grinded in front of them her gaze went straight through him like a hawk. "Tomorrow is the big day" she projected like a robot toying with her glass. Rwanda's head turned slowly like a possessed Halloween doll with widened pupils, mouth still half open.
"Not only will I be the first R&D Head in the world to awaken a Frozen body" she took a deep breath and smiled for the first time in years "I'll be dating a Tomp and can retire to luxury" throwing the contents of her glass efficiently to the back of her throat.

Rwanda was intrigued enough to unstick her arms from the chair and chuckle "Eh I'm not quite sure you're his type mate" she slurred. The chuckle erupted into a hyena like roar. She remembered Lucy's ex-conquests; There was the 8 monther (tall and pale, shaved head, ex-boxer), 6 monther (shaved head too, had a cut scar across his eyelid), 5 monther (paler, with hunched shoulders and quite meek, had a bruised eye once) and the 1 monther (never met him but knew he went to the hospital on their last date).

Lucy, acutely aware Rwanda was correct, vowed, "I'll make sure I am". Man magnet was not exactly on her CV, no relationship had been instigated by the male and none had lasted more than 8 months. At the gates of Cambridge University her mother's encouragement 'focus on your studies, men are only a distraction, this is the start of a prosperous career' was mis-read as 'stick to what you are good at you ugly duckling'.

CHAPTER 8

Everything that creeps upon the ground of every kind

It was Thursday. Alison had selected the white and black silk scarf across her shoulder. Dressing up was second nature, like breathing. The head of legal, the whole research team and her selected loyal favorites from other teams were waiting by the main teleportation hub. There was a beep. He had arrived. The silhouette depicted an impressive tall frame of a confident superior league of man. However when the teleportation light faded they saw it was simply a 20 year old with shabby hair covered in spots. A typical post-teen. Some of the research team exchanged looks and almost smirked, how could such a youth impact their long-standing technology driven business. Alison on the other hand knew to never underestimate an enemy, especially those in politics.

With open arms and a warm smile "As the owner and CEO of Life Beyond I would like to welcome..."
"Lets get on with it, I want to see our president" Dawson abruptly interrupted, whipping his

sunglasses off. No eye contact, just an allusive vacant expression.
Alison maintained her composure and slowly replied, "I understand Mr. Dawson Tomp, we will take you...."
"I meant NOW," his hands snapped onto his childish hips nearly bringing his trousers down, clearly his natural posture. The superhero stance was lost on the others who simply raised eyebrows or rolled their eyes. Some of the team started whispering. Alison blocked this out and escorted Dawson to the fridge.

They were met by all 10 handymen, surrounding the stranger to cautiously protect their treasured working environment and restrict his view. Hired not only as diligent workers, the handymen respected those they guarded and the seriousness of their duties. Lives were at stake. Lucy however had snuck in the back uninvited. Poising her perfectly manicured pale hand over the central computer Alison instructed "Tomp, 20.." interrupted, her gaze shot to the back.
"Good morning Mr. Tomp, I'm Lucy Baker, Head of Research" Unrecognizable Lucy wore a long strawberry blond wig and had painted over all tattoos, tottering on small heels with a bright white smile. While the team was stunned in shock, Dawson remained focused and almost hissed at Alison

"So when will you be able to wake him up?"
Already bored with his behavior, short-dick-syndrome overcompensation, she revealed the screen with her mechanical presentation hand gestures.
"This is a live screening of Mr. Tomp". Dawson snaked towards the screen in apprehension; the strange green glow distorted his relatives old face held up by a dense gel liquid. The sight repulsed him. So human, yet so unnatural. He wondered if the eyes could open any second.

Alison's heart raced as he examined the screen closely, sweat had reached her eyebrows. Lucy's heart raced with embarrassment, her head had lowered significantly to the same height as Alison's bolt upright spine. The team was as silent as the grave, eagerly awaiting some sort of response.

Keen not to disappoint an audience, "So let's wake him up" Dawson proudly announced like a peacock fluttering its feathers.
Alison had prepared for this exact scenario, and no others "I'm afraid it is unsafe to do so, there is a much greater chance of rupturing the vital organs. Therefore under our contract and by law we cannot

permit an awakening" she smirked while reciting the well rehearsed standard company policy line.

"What does THAT mean? I'll get my lawyers on you" Dawson's face erupted in red. His fist clenched too close to Alison's face for comfort.

Alison's smile faded and through gritted teeth she spat out the rest of the company policy lines; "We empathize with your frustration but given the nature of such a critical decision, the power of attorney lies with Life Beyond with oversight from the Global Healthcare Institute and Global Right to Life Laws"

Dawson wasn't listening, no-one ever likes to hear no, let alone a 20 year old with an audience with media and paparazzi drones acutely awaiting back in the US. The petulant child stormed out in a flustered rage, arms swinging violently. The herd of handymen followed to ensure the intruder used the correct tunneled route back to where he came from.

Billy placed his tired hand on Alison's back to comfort her, he knew her too well. While the best outcome had played out and the smiles shone through, both were still scared. This wasn't over, the journey was now simply out of their hands.

ACT 3

CHAPTER 9

You shall have them for food

While all employees followed their routine roles, for Alison the remainder of the day was simply a blur. Drained from the morning stress, she retired to her office sanctuary once the others had clocked-off. It was a Thursday after all, so at 7pm sharp absolutely everyone (except for security) vanished in the blink of an eye to join the teleportation hub queue.

She closed the large door with a heavy sigh. This gigantic office was her refuge, and more of a home than her flat. With the weight of corporate life pressure on her shoulders, exhausted, she edged towards her favorite corner - the darkest area between the wall of family portraits and the wall with the door. While she faced the 30ft high, 40ft wide clear unobscured glass window, she was too far away to see her reflection. She would have seen a scared little girl, cradling herself on the floor with her arms around her legs for support, facing the shiny floor. It was pitch black outside, with clouds blocking all light pollution.

This child-like pose had never improved any situation, but simply delayed it; her father would still be deceased with her at the helm of Life Beyond; she would still be alone and childless at 30, likely forever; she would still have committed those crimes and be punished accordingly. Alison needed to deaden the acute awareness of what would become of her, the future was anything but bright. Almost wanting to freeze herself. As an alternative, she edges towards the decanter, her self-prescribed medicine, in a hidden desk draw and started to drink one, two, three... until it was empty.

Her view was not only clouded by the alcohol, but tears, yet she still felt the watchful eyes of the family portraits. Their smiles and buoyant postures always made her feel like they looked down on her from beyond the grave, constantly judging. "I'm sorry" she moaned with a slur "I've handled more than my fair share, it's not just me who let it down".

Her throat closed. Her eyes sharpened. Her heart stopped for a second. The solution became crystal clear. The way to stop the madness. She had only felt this way once before, 20 May.

CHAPTER 10

Only, you shall not eat flesh with its life, that is, its blood

In the outskirts of London Lucy faced her own truth; She will not be dating one of Tomps elite descendants, or rise to fame by awakening a frozen body. The dream of retiring to luxury had come to an abrupt end.

Decorated in red, black and white mosaic tiles and metallic furniture, her confined flat was almost constructed for the sole purpose of making the occupant lose their mind; so much tiny detail on the curved walls, uneven floor, and frustrating lack of symmetry even among the spotlights. Lucy had tried to combat the unease of her flat with bland white furnishings but over time this morphed into a manic mess, only worsened by the scattered heaps of clothes.

The outskirts were just as busy and loud as the main city; drone speed limits were much higher outside London's congested air space, and their acceleration gave rise to a persistent high pitched whistling noise. Landfill purges to destroy the ever-increasing rubbish occasionally shook the building, accompanied with a strange burning smell.

Yet this was now her home. With no debts, as Head of R&D at a top-firm, her situation was considered luxury for most. Besides what would she do with a slightly larger flat? Even if she had cash to burn, it would still go to dumps like Reids. While she had accepted reality, she was yet to give up on her dream.

The "go hard or go home" mantra echoed in her ear from all those self-help books. However she was at home. That needed to change. Slowly inching her heavy frame up from the sofa her eyes focused on the teleportation hub. A new idea had ignited. As per every morning six days a week, she entered the wide white tube. She applied the eye protection and connection cable (tethering of her feet and arms with magnetic discs – to ensure a limb didn't get lost on the way) before commanding with perfect clarity "Work – reception".

CHAPTER 11

And it was so

Alison had escaped to the 110th floor open roof. Like Babylon, the building was too tall for human control and unapologetically swayed in rhythm to the gale force winds, changing direction at whim above the smog sky layer below. Nothing had been built to endure in this city, man-made or otherwise.

Alison had flung off her shoes. The white uniform started to slightly peel away in the toxic fumes, her hair dusted with grey smoke and her organs were incorrectly balanced – liver filled with one type of toxin, lungs another, stomach completely empty. Giddy with the height, Alison embraced the lonely yet somehow comforting atmosphere. The vastness of the roof immersed her and for a while she was gleefully unaware, skipping towards the edge, laughing in the thick of it all.

"INTRUSION, INTRUSION" the red glowing gloves vibrated. The screeching alarm catapulted her away from the edge in a hurried panic. She clambered back to safety and ran like a mother to defend her newborn.

Lucy, well aware of her restricted security, was repeatedly scanning her arm across the first access gate. "ACCESS DENIED, ACCESS DENIED" the story of her life she thought, again and again. She waited and waited, the silent clock ticking in her mind, knowing the key would arrive eventually.

Staring down the white-boxed glowing corridor, Lucy saw her nemesis emerge. The usual elegant stride, air of importance and poise had vanished. Alison dragged her dirty bare feet up the corridor, approaching in an unusually non-straight line with her head hanging and makeup slightly running. The ocean blue eyes had an irksome glaze. Both knew this was where destiny had brought them tonight, the precise place they needed to be.

"You here to find your wig" Alison teased in a childish high-pitched drunken slurred squeal. Lucy would have rolled her eyes but they remained firmly fixed on the vexing Alison, and dared not deviate for a split second. This condition was unexpected and potentially dangerous. While mindlessly progressing through the access gates with Lucy in tow, both the computer systems and security guards hesitated at each step, but let the leaders pass.

They had entered the unattended Fridge. Blinding white light flooded the immense storage space; Lucy's idea of heaven; order, cleanliness, efficient, purpose built, one central computer. Pausing in admiration, she didn't have time earlier in the day, she felt the impeccably clean air, noted the completely odorless scent and saw her reflection in the pristine almost reflective white floor. Almost skipping like a kid in a candy shop she tapped away at the central computer, ignoring Alison's sloth like pace to the center of the facility.

Lucy innocently mumbled under her breath "What's going on, why don't I have access to Tomp, I have Level 4 clearance?"

"Well lets see clever clogs, what do you think?" Lagging behind but now regaining some composure Alison's hands were flung in exaggeration like a sea-creature's tentacles "What do you think happens when untested, half-baked technology is used waaaaay ahead of its time huh?" Leaning in with a malicious yet teasing tone "You can't even get the Fluid right today!" She went to poke Lucy's shoulder but missed.

Breaking eye contact Alison slowly edged towards the clanking stairs in the corner. Remaining at the computer Lucy checked the sealed exit again in a perplexed panic, then followed the CEO. Alison occasionally tripped on the steps, but reached the top floor, the furthest corner, and shook her arm confidently. "ACCESS GRANTED - COMPARTMENT 502" The computer systems had the same voice as Alison who had designed everything. Only her armband had access. The steel shutter door jumped up in a loud thunder. 100ft long and 30ft high. The large sheet clambered to the ceiling. These gates were built to store, not to open.

CHAPTER 12
In the beginning

Alison was only 18 years old when she inherited one of the most prestigious companies, not just in London, but the world. Already burdened with high expectations, the debts passed on by her father had added another pressure. Ever since she could remember, Life Beyond had been her home. Billy and her father (but mostly Billy) had taught her everything from the technology, the people, the procedures to the finances. She could recite any legislation or company policy in her sleep and often did. While never taking time to reflect on the grave matters of the job, she had earned her business stripes well before her time came.

The facility she inherited in 2267 was at maximum capacity. Each compartment held thousands of freezing pods, stacked like the Alexandria catacombs over each other in light metallic industrial bars. All pre-2100 vintages were held in a single room, with pods sometimes thrown in like a jumble sale given the limited space. Identification methods were poor at best. The storage facility was maintained at exactly zero degrees centigrade.

Only a few months into her new role as CEO, when she was still wearing a mourning band, an unsavory issue emerged. Stressed and slightly depressed, Alison had long blond wavy hair covering her youthful, lily-white face. Her baggy light pink dress had the company logo on the back (hands holding a snowflake) in white, a subtle uniform. Billy caught her after hours when she was locking up her metallic and temporary looking office door. His eyes and cheeks were hollow. In a quiet tremble "I..I...I hear noises... in the facility."

The pair power walked along the uneven floors to the storage unit, Alison brushing her long hair off her face and Billy's quivering arm outstretched pointing to the source of the noise like a magnet.

Everyone had left for the day; all was calm and quiet except for the gentle buzz of the dim hanging lights that made the black and blue floor look like a cracked chessboard. Billy continued to point. Alison was tired and while she cared deeply about the company and Billy, she wanted to simply identify the noise as a fallen pod (after all they were stacked badly) or faulty machinery (a pretty common issue) or just Billy's imagination (he was old after all) and attend her yoga session.

She marched right up to the door. No sound. Putting her ear up the door, she heard it; a strange symphony of whines and groans, people in pain. Slowly rotating her head to Billy, "do you, are they, awake?" The reality had yet to sink in. They stood motionless and rigid, heads both tilted quizzically.

After a long labored pause "Who else has heard these noises?" Alison queried in her feminine high-pitched naive tone. "No-one", he confirmed with reassuring confidence, head still tilted in disbelief and denial. "I'm the only one staying here this late, the systems in the daytime are too loud to hear anything else anyways" further justifying his bold claim.

Like a foot soldier on the battlefield Alison stated unhelpfully "we err, we need to do something" Billy continued to look up for further instruction, but it didn't come. She didn't even blink. He scurried to the cupboard and collected two hand-held torches, a headlight, a crowbar and a knife. She smiled thankfully and took the crowbar and torch, "let's investigate further" she ordered authoritatively with confidence restored, and opened the door.

The humming door mechanics rattled their bones. While only 10 seconds the wait felt like eternity with ever jolt upwards equally startling. Gradually the bitter chemical smell grew. The noise had stopped. The deep black pit felt equally empty and occupied. Barely breathing Alison scanned the room with her torch, tip-toeing into the unknown. She illuminated the scratched floor tiles, a top casket on the racks, and numerous pods piled on top of each other on the floor. The lid seal was broken on one.

With trepidation she examined further. Before she could alert Billy he had run back. The sleeping slumber was over. The dark room murmured with life and Alison saw a yellow eye staring straight through her in the casket. A twisted green arm with boils, bruises and slime firmly grabbed her wrist. Screaming out all the air in her lungs, Alison shuddered backwards, flinging the crowbar for protection. The eye smiled and grip remained undisturbed. Stumbling on the floor she hacked at the arm, black blood oozing out in a haunting high-pitched wail. The eye smiled with pleasure. On the third attempt she was freed, with her eyes streaming and heart pounding "CLOSE THE DOOR", Billy obeyed.

Running through the occupied darkness, Billy saw the creatures chasing the light. Alison's long wavy hair was trapped in another grasp, crashing her body down to the floor. Billy leapt in, the door edging to a close. Hacking away at her hair with his knife they escaped together physically unharmed.

Breathless their bodies crawled away from the closed door. The sound reverberated around the entire building, louder than ever. They had started scratching the door like desperate feral animals.
"They were cannibal." Billy breathed in "started eating each other" breathed in "did you see the ones in the back?" Billy almost fainted.
"Why was the blood black?" Alison's hands clasped on her battered head and slime filled her now short hair, wrapping her brain. While too close to the problem, the solution remained a far-reaching puzzle "They must have reacted with the fluid"
 "They were mutants, like aliens, like ghosts, like.."
"Ghosts?" Alison laughed, "no such thing – they were an experiment gone wrong, that's all", she adamantly shrieked. Her analytical mindset has switched in as a form of survival, protecting her from reality.

Nervous Billy remained seated on the floor "So what now?" Distressingly they didn't know how many of the 78 thousand bodies in that compartment had been woken up, were safely frozen, or been eaten. It was multiple vintages after all. There was an agonizing long pause, with each second the sound seemed to seep further under their skin, etching at their minds.

"There is only one option" Alison murmured with tears caressing her flush face "But it must be humane". No other solutions even came to her mind. After 4 further hours in the lab, they had created the required five toxic gas canisters. Their adrenaline and sense of urgency was balanced by their conscience, resulting in a modest work speed. Edging the shutter door slightly open one last time, they rolled them through the letterbox opening. An hour later, they walked emotionlessly back to their homes until daybreak. The next day the noise had stopped. All staff access passes were changed. Alison would run the company under a firmer grasp. The facility would be held at minus 30 degrees at least.

Over the next year the daily disposal of bodies was done in the dead of night. No teleportation, no witnesses, just Billy and Alison carrying industrial bags of decapitated parts by the river to be shipped off to China as animal feed. It was physically and mentally exhausting work. Crime doesn't pay. The new facility was created to form a new legacy, to house the frozen bodies safely. The new technology was the perfect excuse for making the team redundant, and hiring a less competent and much cheaper finance director who didn't see the missmatch of new pods being brought vs. pods being thrown away as an issue at all. In a world of limited resources the skill of counting became overrated anyway.

Alison became immune to the cutting up of mutants, but the dragging of bodies and scratching on her arms and legs from the caskets made her sick if she ate. Her face became thinned and hollow. Her arms and legs scarred. That eye, those faces, the distorted bodies with missing limbs, extra limbs and sinister smiles haunted her every day and every night. Emaciated, socially cut-off, she resorted to drink and cosmetic drugs to remove the worry lines or any vague clue to the world that all was not as it seemed.

CHAPTER 13

Be fruitful and multiply, and fill the earth

In the new fridge facility, Lucy eagerly scanned the vast compartment 502, but was bewildered when Alison opened a casket. Almost running to the safety of the deceased, she stopped mid-motion. The low sitting pod was empty. Perfectly usable, just perfectly unused.

Alison confessed queerly, "I couldn't have let the company crumble any further."
Still puzzled, Lucy questioned, "Why didn't this go through the research department?"
"Because they were not strictly speaking deceased" Alison spat out hastily. It seemed not to matter who knew anymore, there was no way out. They would come for Tomp and not find him.
"So, so we can wake them up?" The glint in Lucy's eye was met with a startling scream "No-one is ever waking up – ever – this is a morgue, with an R&D department to help cure current diseases and investment arm to keep the company afloat – that's it! It's not safe! You didn't see what I saw!"

Lucy barks back with rage, towering over Alison "Don't act all moral with me you blonde, entitled bitch"
"You're the freak with a fascination of death, I know what they say about you, dirty man-beater man-eater!" In a crazed intuitive reaction Lucy grabbed Alison by the throat. Both shocked by the abrupt action, Lucy pushed her enemy into the casket before any time to resist. Slamming down the lid, Alison's hand was caught on the edge; after a further slam the blood soaked hand retreated into the unit. Sealing shut Lucy drowned out the screams with the clattering close of the shutter door, leaving one living creature trapped in the otherwise empty morgue.

Jumping down the long five flights of stairs, enthralled by the experience Lucy licks her lips as Alison's screams die down into white noise. Tingling with excitement she searched for someone to wake up on the central screen; perhaps another US political candidate? Lucy envisaged herself as a true hero, she would still be the first person to wake up the frozen. June will do. She knew this had been her purpose all along.

While not in her work remit, locating the pod on the first floor was quick and easy. Compartment Gate 106 was available to her security access. Lucy's smug expression solidified, relieved she had access to this gate – a good sign. The shiny white pod was elegant and almost beautiful in its simplicity, with the twenty-digit identification code beautifully engraved in the otherwise perfect shiny cocoon. The weight caused Lucy to cry out and she heaved it across the floor. The workmen packed away all the trolleys for the day and she didn't have access to the lifts. Her athletic build was sweating and aching. With one last push she thrust the pod down the stairs. It crashed into the door of the analysis unit. Lucy regained her breath. Almost giddy from the physical effort, the real work had only just begun. Shaking, she weakly wiped her sweaty hands on the grubby jacket before hooking up the pod to the system; connecting the tubes, charging the pod, collecting fluid pressure data. Every cell in Lucy's body was electrified yet terrified. This was the moment for both Lucy and June.

Unknown to all but the CEO, when the fridge is accessed outside hours, Alison and also Billy's wristbands sound an alarm, summoning them to the fridge. The sleepy guardian Billy had teleported to work in a daze. Passing each access gate to the fridge was like counting sheep; every gate passing would lower the eyelids a tad further. This marathon of a walk was enough for one day, a certainly too much at mid-night for the 113 year old. Given the importance of the day, he expected to see Alison buzzing around the fridge, checking the systems, going over it again and again, almost hoping there is a failure and she's found out. He often visited his theory that she may have been happier if she'd publicized the whole ordeal. She could have blamed it on Graham and everyone would have believed her. The company would have surely survived, there would always be a macabre desire for body freezing, whether the science worked or not.

Arriving at last to what felt like home, he was coldly shocked to see movement in the lab. He cautiously trundled closer and was surprised to see a red head of hair flying around in such a fury. His face was pressed firmly against the glass window, enlarging his eyes and nose, removing all his wrinkles. The wild fish inside the glass bowl didn't even realize.

Almost screeching like a teenage girl, Lucy merrily hummed while watching the progress bar on the 'de-freeze' screen. It was better than any movie. It reached 100%. Unsealing the lid, Lucy slowly opened the dried chamber, savoring every moment. Billy was bewitched and gazed into the dry ice smoke. A cold chill evaporated into the atmosphere. Once acclimatized to the sight of the frail white body, Lucy measured the pulse methodically. She measured the pulse. She tried to find the pulse. She tried to find any pulse. Lifting the wet arm it dropped out the pod brushing motionlessly past her leg. No movement. She lifted it again. The dead arm dropped again, splattering some fluid to the floor. Bewildered and breathless Lucy staggered backwards knocking the cables in despair. She bit her nails until her fingers bled. The screen went red.

Horrified Billy silently scurried-away, vowing to report the incident first thing tomorrow. As he approached the second access gate on his exit, the masked faceless armed guard stopped him.
"Is Alison OK?" his concern showed through the voice. The guards wore more protection and padding than the police, although perhaps this was for warmth too, in deep blue shiny uniforms. Every inch was covered in layers except for their thumbs to use for identification.
"Is Alison here?" Billy checked.

"Yes she let Lucy in, she was in quite a state, I know it's not my place but we didn't even know if we should let them in" Billy rubbed the guards arm, which stood several feet above his head, in gratitude. Now he was worried. Now he must investigate thoroughly.

Skating stealthily across the frictionless floor he approached the central computer. Blinking heavily to focus his tired eyes. Compartment 502 had been opened and closed. 502!! No one was ever allowed in there, only he and Alison had access. Was she trying to jeopardies all we worked for? Surely after all those nights of sawing, hacking, black blood spilling and dragging industrial coffins was something she wanted to black-out and never address again, even with this Tomp business?

Now in frustration he approached the dreaded Gate 502. His breathing had become labored. Creeping to the door he hears a faint wailing. Muscle memory sprang his frail body backwards. He sank to the floor and held his head "No...No..No. It can't be happening. Not again...No...No" Hands over his ears he cradled back and forth on the floor with terrified tears. He couldn't suppress the memory, not even after this long. The trauma would always remain.

He lurched forward in an attempt to flee the scene but stumbled. Repeating the lurch, he stumbled again. Blinded by the light he hears a faint "Help me, help me please, I'm trapped" he ran down the stairs spooked, mouth gaping like a fish out of water for air.

In the corner of his now enlarged eyes he catches Lucy in the ground floor lab with tubes in her teeth, connecting everything and anything to the corpse in a franticly desperate attempt to change nature. A strange knot in Billy stomach drew him away from the scene, back up the stairs. He didn't want to witness those awful rumors about Lucy.

He knew he needed to face his fears one day and this was it. Commanding Gate 502 to open, the whining "help" sound grew louder. The gleaning red blood in the otherwise pristine white room caused Billy to almost vomit. The smell of blood was sickeningly sweet. It was fresh, and still bleeding from the inside. Squinting through closed eyes and tense muscles, Billy took a deep breath, murmured a quick prayer, and released the lid.

Gulping for air Alison sprung up in surprise like a jack in the box. Billy almost threw her back in with the force of his embrace. "Thank you, thank you Billy," she cried, relieved, feeling blessed with the gift of life. Billy chuckled in bewildered relief. While his mouth moved no words came out, and his eyes darted all around her in surprise. Their gaze was all he needed, he had been more like family than anyone else in her life and she cherished him. She held his head against hers, and their tears met each other before they hugged again.

Snapping back into survival mode, Alison used her originally light blue scarf as a makeshift bandage, they charged to her office after creeping past the lab. She may have lost a lot of blood but her head was still screwed on very tight. A phone call had to be made. Almost fainting as she reached the desk, her shaking non-bandaged hand pressed the hologram call button. Billy held back and waited behind a totem pole.

"Mr. Prime Minister, I'm sorry to call at such an hour, but I have some rather unfortunate news. It concerns two US politicians" Alison leant over her desk; her hologram message would mask the blood, dirt, and deadness of her eyes. Instead he would hear her slow paced voice as 'composed' rather than exhausted, her stance as 'authoritative' rather than struggling to stand. For once she had a scapegoat, and she wanted to play this card when she was one step ahead, before it was too late. There must only be one side to the story.

The Prime Minister never liked being woken up, he always needed his sleep to think clearly. It should be called 'brain sleep' rather than 'beauty sleep' he always thought. No one ever looked beautiful first thing in the morning. In this case it was obvious what should be done, he just needed to make one phone call to the US Embassy, give them Lucy's details and then go back to bed. Problem solved both swiftly and according to the book. He never questioned any facts that Alison provided.

CHAPTER 14

Let them have dominion over the fish of the sea, and over the birds of the air, and over the cattle, and over all the wild animals of the earth, and over every creeping thing that creeps upon the earth

In the lab no stone was left unturned, Lucy attempted everything and anything. The corpse remained soulless. After two further hours she slumped to the floor in defeat. Her eyes dry from the lack of blinking. Her skin flaking with dryness despite the clammy sweat. Accepting her failure she returned the pod to its slumber chamber and herself to hers.

Arriving at her flat in a haze, she didn't turn on the lights, or have dinner or take a shower or write her diary she had hoped one day to publish as an autobiography as per her normal routine. Blubbering to herself through the tears she beelined to bed. Collapsing in a heap, she twisted onto her back with eyes and mouth wide-open, struggling for breath. She didn't focus on the fire alarm on the ceiling as per her normal routine either but starred into oblivion.

She had devoted her whole life to work, to this sole achievement of awaking a frozen body. She longed for closure on what was on the other side. Where really was her father when he left this earth all those years ago? Lucy hated her mother for that fatal night in the kitchen, even if it really was self defense, how could Phil be that evil. While only around for the first four years of her life, Lucy missed him dearly. He looked and sounded just like her, they even had the same laugh. She knew for certain she would have been happy if she had a father, and not just her self-absorbed selfish mother who never understood her or even tried to. Would he have told her what to do now? Should she have tried something else? Or never even tried anything?

Shaking with tears the cogs in her brain started to get back to work. How could she be so stupid as to believe Alison? Oh my God what will happen to Alison in the fridge!? What time is it? What do I do now? I can't leave the UK, or can I? What would I do for money? As she jerked upright in panic a camouflaged US policeman was thrusting a black bag over her head and injected her arm. At least sleep came easy now.

It took three hours for the effect of the drugs to leave Lucy's giant ox-like body. Slowly adjusting she came to terms with her situation; tied with electric netting to a chair, under a spotlight in an otherwise pitch-dark room. Struggling to breathe in the cool silent air, her wrists and ankles were in sharp shooting pain from the electric current. She tasted blood in her mouth. Looking up into the pitch darkness she knew she was being watched but no one was there. As her eyes began to focus she saw in the distance a large American Flag lit up. She knew this was bad situation that was only going to get worse, she had been taken prisoner to the US. An automated voice echoed in the darkness.
"Lucy Barker, you are charged with murder of Mr. Tomp and Ms. June through clinical negligence and unlawful attempts to awaken frozen bodies. You are sentenced to the chair" Confused and petrified, the black bag returned to stifle any reply. Her body was escorted with no sense of dignity to a separate set of forces.

On the other side of the video link, the Judge unclicked the telecom button with his fat finger in

the plush office only a few miles north of Washington and switched the screen from 'Live Prison - 8485' to 'Meeting Agenda Document', moving down the action list. All twelve committee members sat comfortably around the round smooth mahogany table in padded armchairs. In between the large screens on the walls were tapestries of the American Flag and hanging gold ornaments. Baskets of refreshments sat in the center of the table, as these daily meetings lasted over 9 hours straight with no interruption from outside. The agenda was always centered around threats to the US, and the Lucy Barker emergency agenda item in particular was a large threat if it got out to the press. Just before starting on the next agenda item, a Committee Member added
"What do we tell the public now, they are expecting Tomp to be woken up?" their bald head slightly sweating with the effort to speak up "And when they find out he is dead, they will simply ask for the daughter"

All Members shifted into thinking positions that varied from either rubbing their double chins, shifting in the grooved seats or tilting their heads. With a sigh the Chairman concluded "We should simply end this frozen body business, we've never faced this kind of public demand before and I don't think it will go away – we don't have enough to distract them with" While silent the room filled with concern.

The newest Committee Member saw an opportunity, for the first time that week, to demonstrate her insight. Tossing her bouncing brunette trusses backwards to show her wide square spectacles covering nearly her whole face "well, all the frozen body facilities are in London, so it can be a random regional power failure glitch". They all gazed in horror at her but dared not comment. This job paid far too well. Upsetting the Chairman was a risk never worth taking. The butterfly effect would occur in any role of responsibility, every single action has a wide range of reactions, so after all who ever really knows if they made a right or wrong decision. The agenda item was ticked off.

CHAPTER 15

Whoever sheds the blood of a human; by a human shall that person's blood be shed

Meanwhile in Prison 8485, an officer was reciting from their manual to sentenced prisoner Lucy Barker. The process was always rushed; the Judge had punished the officer previously for a 5-minute delay, as within that time the prisoner had spoken which legally means they have to go through court and a formal trial. "While we try to minimize any discomfort, there will be a mild sting for a few seconds. My trusted clinicians will take you through to the chair with your regional Ambassador" Lucy's black bag was removed and replaced seamlessly with a gas mask. A few bodies were busily working around her, carrying out their routine duties. For once her mind didn't punish her for all the things she never achieved, the dreams unfulfilled, but rewarded her with the memories of all she had learnt, all she had gained, all she had earned in her few years. A gentle smile broke out. She may not have won, but she knew she had played the game of life well. Now she could see if anything really did lie beyond the known world and if her father was waiting.

It was 2am in London. The vast headquarters of Life Beyond were still occupied by the CEO. Alison suddenly felt a chill dance down her spine. She spun round. No one was there, yet her unlit office felt taken with an unwanted ghost. Was it her grandfather again? She felt his presence in vulnerable times although knew it could be her overactive imagination. Or was it Lucy taking revenge? Alison didn't want to think about it, she had to make that call, there was no other way. There was just far too much to lose, millions relied on Life Beyond either directly or indirectly and needed Alison as the sole heir to guide the ship, who else would? It was her or Lucy and while not an ideal outcome it was the only choice in Alison's eyes. The only option. It was fair after all as she did kill June. Lucy was always a bitch anyway who got what she deserved surely. The sting of guilt and regret still clutched every inch of Alison's skin, the power of which she knew from experience would not decay with time.

Alison cradled her whisky glass like a baby in her unharmed hand while leaning against her desk, the ice cubes clattering. The alcohol felt so much stronger this evening or perhaps her legs were shaking for another reason. Her feet were bruised and still grubby from outside. The blue scarf and half her white dress had stained dark red through and through from the blood. Even the black toxic rain outside attacking London somehow appeared red. Sheets of water were falling from the sky, the only sound in the vast space. Quietness reminded Alison of her loneliness. Why did he leave her?

In a deranged state of despair, Alison gazed up into the night as the city paused, pressing her head on the window. Smiling she remembered singing with her grandfather at his tin-like office "Incy wincey spider climbing up the water spout, down came the rain and washed the spider out, out came the sunshine and washed up all the rain, and the incy wincey spider climbed up the spout again". It was meant to give her motivation to fight another day, but it was never as inspiring as whisky. She went to pour another glass.

All of a sudden the US Threat Protection Committee's secret plan was enforced. The power was cut for the whole city. All went dark across London. Confused, Alison pinched her face, had she passed out again?

The energy supply had gone all across London, there was nothing to be seen outside. She swooned to the desk screen - even the backup had gone. She tried again - why had the second energy backup gone? One Mississippi, two Mississippi, three Mississippi's of time with no energy supply was enough to fail the entire fridge system. She counted on her shaking bloody fingers - this blackout lasted ten Mississippi's. Alison dropped her glass, smashing on the floor to a thousand pieces, cutting her pale legs. She only felt fear. More blood was spilt that night.

Opening the office door to the left was the route to the lift and therefore access to the roof, to the right was the corridor to the fridge, straight ahead was teleportation to anywhere she could imagine. There was one thing to do first, she left a password protected video message "Billy…….. I can't imagine where I would be without you….. It goes without saying that you have been more like a father ….. You've done so much for me. I'm so sorry to let you down. I just can't…I just… can't keep …..this – I'm instigating Code Black, you know where to find me"

THE END...

Let's Continue the Conversation

EMACACORY   .COM

Printed in Great Britain
by Amazon